# ear Parent:
## ur child's love of reading starts here!

ry child learns to read in a different way and at his or her own
ed. Some go back and forth between reading levels and read
rite books again and again. Others read through each level in
er. You can help your young reader improve and become more
fident by encouraging his or her own interests and abilities. From
ks your child reads with you to the first books he or she reads
ne, there are I Can Read Books for every stage of reading:

## SHARED READING
Basic language, word repetition, and whimsical illustrations,
ideal for sharing with your emergent reader

## BEGINNING READING
Short sentences, familiar words, and simple concepts
for children eager to read on their own

## READING WITH HELP
Engaging stories, longer sentences, and language play
for developing readers

## READING ALONE
Complex plots, challenging vocabulary, and high-interest topics
for the independent reader

## ADVANCED READING
Short paragraphs, chapters, and exciting themes
for the perfect bridge to chapter books

Can Read Books have introduced children to the joy of reading
ce 1957. Featuring award-winning authors and illustrators and a
ulous cast of beloved characters, I Can Read Books set the
ndard for beginning readers.

lifetime of discovery begins with the magical words **"I Can Read!"**

*Visit www.icanread.com for information*
*on enriching your child's reading experience.*

# I Can Read!

READING 2 WITH HELP

**DreamWorks SHREK THE THIRD**

A Good King Is Hard to Find

Shrek the Third: A Good King Is Hard to Find  Shrek is a registered trademark of DreamWorks Animation L.L.C.  Shrek the Third ™ &
© 2007 DreamWorks Animation L.L.C.  All rights reserved. No part of this book may be used or reproduced in any manner whatsoever
without written permission except in the case of brief quotations embodied in critical articles and reviews. Printed in the United States
of America. For information address HarperCollins Children's Books, a division of HarperCollins Publishers, 1350 Avenue of the
Americas, New York, NY 10019. www.harpercollinschildrens.com

Library of Congress catalog card number: 2007920952
ISBN-10: 0-06-122866-4 — ISBN-13: 978-0-06-122866-7

❖     First Edition

# DREAMWORKS
# SHREK THE THIRD

## A Good King Is Hard to Find

Adapted by Catherine Hapka

Illustrations by Steven E. Gordon

HarperCollins*Publishers*

The kingdom of Far Far Away
needs a new king.
Shrek and Fiona are next in line
for the throne.

But Shrek does not want the job.

"There must be somebody else,"

he says.

"Anybody?"

There's only one way out.
Shrek must find Fiona's cousin,
a kid named Arthur Pendragon.
Artie can be king instead.

Shrek says good-bye to Fiona
and sets off on another adventure
with his best friends,
Donkey and Puss In Boots.

Soon they find Artie.

He doesn't look much like a king,

but Shrek doesn't care.

"Come on, Your Majesty," says Shrek

"Let's get you fitted for your crown."

s classmates laugh.

ing?" they say.

Iore like the Mayor of Loserville!"

Artie turns toward the crowd.

"So long, guys," he says.

"Have fun in class while I run a kingdo

Artie follows Shrek onto the ship.

They set sail for Far Far Away.

"You'll love being king,"
Shrek tells Artie.
"You'll have chefs making you fancy fo
says Donkey.

d you'll have royal tasters

ou won't get poisoned," Puss adds.

ur royal bodyguards will keep you safe,"

; Donkey.

ison? Bodyguards? Stop the boat!"

s Artie.

Artie grabs the wheel

to turn the ship around.

"I'm going back!" he cries.

"Back to being a loser?" Shrek asks.

Then he feels terrible.

Shrek and Artie fight to control the ship. They end up crashing it instead.

When they get to shore,
the group finds an old wizard
named Merlin.
He used to be Artie's teacher.

Merlin performs a magic spell.
It sends Artie and the others
straight back to Far Far Away.

Shrek thinks his problems are over.

Then he gets a look at Far Far Away.

The evil Prince Charming

has almost taken over the kingdom.

Artie thinks the city looks terrible.

"It wasn't like this when we left,"

Shrek tells him.

They find Shrek's friend, Pinocchio.

"The villains have taken over!" he says.

Pinocchio points to a poster for a play

The poster shows Charming defeating Sh

Shrek and his friends

talk their way into the castle.

They have to stop Charming!

Shrek and Artie find Prince Charming

Charming laughs at Artie.

Artie turns to Shrek.

"Go away, kid.

There's nothing you can do," says Shr

ter Artie leaves the room,

arming captures Shrek.

s almost time for the play to start!

"Ladies and gentlemen,"

Charming says to the crowd.

"Welcome to my happily-ever-after."

He points his sword at Shrek.

A bright light hits the stage.

"Hold it!" yells Artie from above.

He grabs a rope and swings to the floor.

Charming and his villains want to figh[t]

But Artie has a better idea.

"Do you really want to be villains

forever?" he asks the bad guys.

"Don't you ever wish

you could be something else?"

The villains like what they hear.

They turn against Charming.

Now Charming will never be king!

Artie used to feel like a loser.

But now he feels smart and strong.

Maybe he is fit to be king, after all

Shrek holds out the crown.

"It's yours if you want it,"

he tells Artie.

"But this time, it's your choice."

Artie smiles and puts on the crown.

His new subjects cheer and shout.

"Artie! Artie! Artie!"

yells the crowd.